LEO
the
Lightning Bug

For all of my people, but especially Sivan, whose adorable message inspired this book's title and author. — E.D.

www.kidwick.com

Copyright 2004 Kidwick Books LLC

Voices on CD (alphabetically):
Benjamin Drachman (Danny), Eric Drachman (Narrator, Oscar), Jonathan Drachman (Uncle Bill), Anton Piatigorsky (Dad), Sivan Piatigorsky-Roth (Patricia), Ava Roth (Mom)

"Procession and Entrance" by George Frideric Handel courtesy of Hyperion Records, Ltd, London
The King's Consort; Robert King, conductor

Scherzo by Gregor Piatigorsky courtesy of The Piatigorsky Foundation
Evan Drachman, cello; Richard Dowling, piano

Text design and layout by Andrew Leman. Set in Providence Sans and Julius Klinger.

Illustrations were painted with gouache on textured boards.

Publisher's Cataloging-in-Publication
(Provided by Cassidy Cataloguing Services, Inc.)

Drachman, Eric.

It's me! / by Eric Drachman ; illustrated by Isabelle Decencière. --
Los Angeles, CA : Kidwick Books, 2004.

p. ; cm. + 1 sound disc.

Ages: 3-7.
CD contains the story, accompanied by sound effects.
Summary: Patricia's joyful creativity is infectious as she takes on different roles in her lively game of dress-up. When she finally appears as herself, however, her family realizes that she's the "real" Patricia, making way for a happy reunion.
ISBN 978-0-9703809-2-0

1. Role playing--Juvenile fiction. 2. Costume--Juvenile fiction. 3. Children's audiobooks. I. Decencière, Isabelle. II. Title.

PZ7.D733 187 2004   2004092008
[E]--dc22   0410

Printed in Korea by Amica Inc., September 24, 2012
Distributed by National Book Network
Published in Los Angeles, CA U.S.A. by Kidwick Books LLC

IT'S ME!

By Eric Drachman

Illustrated by Isabelle Decencière

Kidwick books

Patricia was the most beautiful girl in the world. She had warm brown eyes and curly dark hair which she loved to brush in the big mirror in her private chambers. She was kind and generous and everyone adored her — all of her people.

Today, her name was Princess Finula-Lily.
She wore a sparkling royal dress and a tiara
covered with priceless, shimmering jewels.
Her trusted dressers had misplaced her
long white princess gloves, so instead,
she wore her big winter mittens.

Princess Finula-Lily made
her way down the stairway,
through the grand hallway,

and paused in the
dining room to gather
her composure for
her regal entrance.
She took a breath...

...then stepped inside
the kitchen where her
people were waiting.

There was a gasp as she flowed in. Oscar barked and jumped on her. There was a round of applause in appreciation of her grace and beauty.

"Welcome, Princess Finula-Lulu,"
Uncle Bill began.

"It's Princess Finula-Lily,"
corrected Princess Finula-Lily.

"Well, what a beautiful
princess you are!"
beamed Mom.

"Beautiful!" agreed
Dad. "I love your
crown."

"Tiara," corrected
the princess.

"Where's Patricia?" asked Uncle Bill.

"I don't know Patricia. I'm Princess Finula-Lily and I'm very very beautiful and everybody loves me."

All of a sudden,
Patricia had an idea.
"Oh, I know!"
she thought —

— and dashed upstairs.

A few minutes later, the door to the kitchen swung open, and standing there was one scary witch.

"Who's that?!?"
gulped Uncle Bill.
"I'm scared."

"It's Patricia," blurted her brother, Danny, "in another costume!" and the dog licked his face till he giggled.

"Well, she's about as tall as Patricia, but my niece does not have that big crooked nose or that pointy black hat. Hmm... what's your name, witch?"

"I'm Pa— I'm Patr—   umm... Patrooshka! ...the evil witch of... um... Maple Court! ...and I'm very very ugly and everyone's afraid of me!"

And she laughed a scary laugh to prove it.

"Don't turn us into toads!" begged Dad.

"Well, you just better be careful," warned Patrooshka, "because that one I already turned into a DOGGY!"

And with a twirl of her
cape, she disappeared
out the door.

Before long, the door swung open again and standing there was Mom's dress — with a little girl inside.

"Who are you?" asked Dad.

"Don't be silly, dear. I'm the mommy and this is our baby, 'Patricia'. Isn't she beautiful when she sleeps?"

"Yes, she is... honey," smiled Dad. "You're doing such a good job raising her!"

"Yes, Patricia is the smartest, kindest, most beautiful girl in the world."

On hearing that, Danny pretended to throw up.

Little Mommy turned around, and on her way out, explained, "I have to go write a new book. I'm a very famous writer, you know."

A few minutes later, the
door swung open again.

"Wow!" gasped Uncle Bill.
"Who's that stylish girl?"

"It's me," answered Patricia, and she sat down on the floor to play with Oscar and Danny.

"Oh, I know," guessed Dad. "You're the farmer's daughter, just back from milking the cows!"

"It's me," corrected Patricia, standing up again.

"I know," said Mom. "You're the girl from that TV show we love so much!"

"It's me!!!" exclaimed Patricia, getting a little frustrated.

"I know," said Danny. "It's the ghost who keeps stealing my toys!"

"It's me!" yelled Patricia, stamping her foot. "It's me!"

"It's you?" asked Mom.
"My wonderful daughter?"

"It's me," said Patricia, and
she hugged her mom.

"I missed you."

"I missed you, too,
sweetheart," grinned
Mom, and she gave
Patricia a great big squeeze.

"I kind of miss that Princess Fool-a-balloo!" teased Danny.

"Finula-Lily!"

laughed everyone...

and they laughed

and laughed.